DATE DUE

JUN 6 '02		

j
Fic Orgel, Doris
Org The mouse who wanted
     to marry
                    [12.00]

JUN 6 '02

STUTSMAN COUNTY LIBRARY
910 5TH ST. S.E.
JAMESTOWN, ND 58401

STUTSMAN COUNTY LIBRARY
BOOKMOBILE
Books for Everyone

DEMCO

ABOUT THE BANK STREET READY-TO-READ SERIES

Seventy years of educational research and innovative teaching have given the Bank Street College of Education the reputation as America's most trusted name in early childhood education.

Because no two children are exactly alike in their development, we have designed the *Bank Street Ready-to-Read* series in three levels to accommodate the individual stages of reading readiness of children ages four through eight.

- ○ *Level 1:* GETTING READY TO READ—read-alouds for children who are taking their first steps toward reading.

- ● *Level 2:* READING TOGETHER—for children who are just beginning to read by themselves but may need a little help.

- ○ *Level 3:* I CAN READ IT MYSELF—for children who can read independently.

Our three levels make it easy to select the books most appropriate for a child's development and enable him or her to grow with the series step by step. The *Bank Street Ready-to-Read* books also overlap and reinforce each other, further encouraging the reading process.

We feel that making reading fun and enjoyable is the single most important thing that you can do to help children become good readers. And we hope you'll be a part of Bank Street's long tradition of learning through sharing.

The Bank Street College of Education

To Emily and her husband
"just right"
—D.O.
For my mom and dad
—H.H.

THE MOUSE WHO WANTED TO MARRY

A Bantam Little Rooster Book/June 1993

Little Rooster is a trademark of Bantam Books,
a division of Bantam Doubleday Dell Publishing Group, Inc.

Series graphic design by Alex Jay/Studio J

Special thanks to James A. Levine, Betsy Gould,
Diane Arico, and Herb Spiers.

Library of Congress Cataloging-in-Publication Data

Orgel, Doris.
The mouse who wanted to marry / by Doris Orgel;
illustrated by Holly Hannon.
p.   cm.—(Bank Street ready-to-read)
"A Byron Preiss book."
"A Bantam Little Rooster book."
Summary: After asking the sun, a cloud,
the wind, and a wall to marry her,
a mouse finds just the right husband.
ISBN 0-553-09235-9 (hc).—ISBN 0-553-37143-6 (tp)
[1. Folklore. 2. Mice—Folklore. 3. Marriage—Folklore.]
I. Hannon, Holly, ill. II. Title. III. Series.
PZ8.1.059Mo 1993
92-10741   CIP   AC

Published simultaneously in the United States and Canada

Bantam Books are published by Bantam Books, a division of Bantam Doubleday
Dell Publishing Group, Inc. Its trademark, consisting of the words "Bantam Books"
and the portrayal of a rooster, is Registered in U.S. Patent and Trademark Office
and in other countries. Marca Registrada. Bantam Books, 1540 Broadway, New
York, New York 10036.

PRINTED IN THE UNITED STATES OF AMERICA

0 9 8 7 6 5 4 3 2 1

Bank Street Ready-to-Read™

The Mouse Who Wanted to Marry

by Doris Orgel
Illustrated by Holly Hannon

A Byron Preiss Book

A BANTAM LITTLE ROOSTER BOOK
NEW YORK · TORONTO · LONDON · SYDNEY · AUCKLAND

"I want to marry,"
said a fine young mouse.
She knew what she wanted:
a husband just right,
good and strong,
and always there
to keep her company.

So the mouse set out to look for one.
The sun shone down and warmed her.
"Sun," said the mouse,
"you are good and strong.
You are always there.
Will you marry me?"

"I am not that strong,"
said the sun.
"I cannot always be there.
See that cloud
with the curly edges?
That cloud will chase me away."

Sure enough,
along came the cloud
and chased the sun away.

"Cloud," said the mouse,
"you are stronger than the sun.
You can always be there.
Will you marry me?"

"The wind is stronger,"
said the cloud.
"Watch. See what happens."

The wind puffed up his cheeks, and
WHHHHH!
He blew the cloud away.

"Wind," said the mouse,
"you are stronger than the cloud.
Surely you can
always be there.
Will you marry me?"

"See that wall?"
asked the wind.
"That wall is stronger
than I am.
Watch."

The wind gusted up
and blew himself at the wall.
The wall hurled him back.
The wind could not blow
through that wall.
So he blew himself away.

"Wall," said the mouse,
"you are stronger than the wind.
Surely, surely
you can always be there.
Will you marry me?"

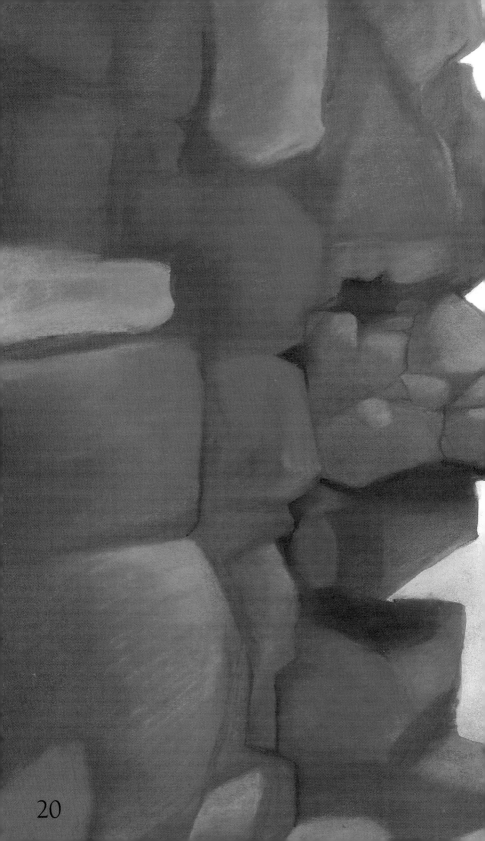

"I am weak,"
said the wall.
"I am full of chinks and holes
where little creatures live.
They nibble, and I crumble.
They are stronger.
They will still be here
long after I am gone."

21

And sure enough,
there came a nibbling
and a crumbling.
A hole opened up.
And who do you think leaped ou
but a fine young mouse!

23

This mouse was stronger
than the wall,
and the wall was stronger
than the wind,
and the wind was stronger
than the cloud,
and the cloud was stronger
than the sun.
So—
this mouse was the strongest
of all!

Besides, he was handsome,
with sparkling eyes,
and silver-gray fur
smooth as velvet.

25

She was so glad to see him!
He was glad to see her, too.
They put their paws around each other.
"Oh, mouse, mouse," they both said,
"you are the mouse for me!"

Soon they married.
They chose the coziest
hole in the wall for their home.

They gathered crunchy pine nuts,
and acorn cups for sipping rain,

and soft, warm feathers for a bed.
They were just right for each other.

31

They still are, to this day.